# The Fifth Floor

pkb Neidlinger

Bloomington, IN

authorHOUSE®

Milton Keynes, UK

*AuthorHouse™*
*1663 Liberty Drive, Suite 200*
*Bloomington, IN 47403*
*www.authorhouse.com*
*Phone: 1-800-839-8640*

*AuthorHouse™ UK Ltd.*
*500 Avebury Boulevard*
*Central Milton Keynes, MK9 2BE*
*www.authorhouse.co.uk*
*Phone: 08001974150*



*First published by AuthorHouse 11/22/2006*

*ISBN: 978-1-4259-5954-8 (sc)*

*Library of Congress Control Number: 2006909596*

*Printed in the United States of America*
*Bloomington, Indiana*

*This book is printed on acid-free paper.*

# Dedication

*This book is dedicated to my parents. Their true love and devotion for each other has enabled them to overcome the numerous obstacles that have been put before them over the last ten years.*

# *Forward*

*Thank you to my family for their support and encouragement during the writing of this book. A special thank you to my children, Aly and Nick, for encouraging me and reminding me to do what I teach my own students to do everyday.*

*Set Goals*
*Believe in Yourself*
*Give It Your Best Shot*

*I love you,*
*Mom*

# Contents

# Chapter 1

Toby stepped frantically into his other black high-top tennis shoe and bolted out the front door toward the bus stop screaming, "Stop! Stop!"

"Toby, hurry!" shouted Mr. Bennett as the chrome yellow school bus came to a screeching halt. Toby's best friends, Jordan, Jeremiah, and Reggie, awaited anxiously as Toby sped toward them on his Deluxe 225XR Flyer Skateboard. The wind splintered through his blonde, moussed, spiked hair as he approached the bus stop just one short block from his home. Toby's mom waved good-bye from the front deck that encircled their red cedar two story home on Dora Avenue.

"See you tonight, Mom!" exclaimed Toby skidding to an abrupt stop.

Bus #18 arrived every day at precisely 7:43 a.m. at the corner of Dora and Virginia Avenue. The bus driver, Mr. Bennett, had been driving bus for twenty-five years. He was everyone's favorite bus driver. His dark gray hair was curled slightly above the ear and his gold-rimmed bi-focal glasses camouflaged his hazel green eyes.

"Toby, you're late again," grinned Reggie as Toby packed his skateboard in his black, oversized gym bag.

"I know," chuckled Toby.

"Mr. Bennett almost didn't stop for you this time," Reggie continued.

"Let's go, Toby!!" commanded Mr. Bennett, "on the bus, NOW!"

"Good morning, Mr. Bennett. What a beautiful October morning," Toby announced as he promenaded down the aisle to the back seat of the bus.

"Sit down, Toby! I'm five minutes behind

schedule thanks to you!" scolded Mr. Bennett.

"Sit down, Toby!" shouted the chorus of students.

"You should be nice to Mr. Bennett, Toby. He's getting old."

"He doesn't care, Jordan. He's just kidding around with me."

"Look, there's Alyssa Williams," pointed Jordan. "She's looking at you, Toby."

"She's not looking at me. She's staring at the new kid in the third seat. Besides, Alyssa only likes me for my brains."

"Who is that new kid?" questioned Jeremiah.

"I heard he moved here from Louisville. His older brother is 6'5" and plays tackle on the high school football team," noted Jordan.

"How old is this kid?.......... He's huge!" stuttered Toby.

"We're here!" interrupted Reggie as he jumped up from his green vinyl seat.

"See you later, Mr. Bennett!" the boys screamed, jumping from the top step of the bus.

"Have a good day!" Mr. Bennett replied as he watched the boys race for the oak framed front doors of Sabens Middle School.

Sabens was the oldest school in Austin. Austin had a modest population of 10,000 people and was nestled among the foothills along the Ohio River. Sabens was the only middle school in Austin. It had been built in the early 1940's and hadn't been remodeled for over twenty-five years. The white tiled floors of the school were accented by orange and blue painted walls. Most of the classrooms had walls, but some of them were more contemporary with only partitions as dividers between classes. Sabens had a regiment of veteran teachers that together had taught for more than 250 years. Most of the students had parents and even grandparents that were schooled at Sabens.

"Good morning, Miss Foley," shouted Toby as

he entered the front doors.

"Good morning, Miss Foley," echoed Jordan.

"Good morning, boys," Miss Foley retorted sternly.

Miss Foley had been the principal for twenty years. No one was really sure when she'd be retiring or if she ever would. Her long wavy black hair was secured tightly behind her ears with tiny gold hairpins. She was a smart dresser. Each day she wore a colorful scarf that flowed gently around her neck and over her left shoulder. She owned an array of pumps that she coordinated with her oval interchangeable framed glasses.

"Hi, Toby!"

"Oh, hi, Alyssa," blushed Toby from behind his locker door. Toby looked around to make sure no one saw him talking to her. Alyssa was the most popular girl in the seventh grade. She lived in the mansion in Austin. Alyssa's family had lived there for over a hundred years. The five gothic scone pillars graced the marble entrance way to the three story, twenty-two room mansion that set atop Hickory Hill overlooking the banks of the Ohio River. Alyssa's family, the Williams, owned several clothing stores nationwide. It was not uncommon for Alyssa to be escorted to school by her limousine driver, Michel, or to go on weekend ski trips to Colorado. Alyssa tried to be a normal twelve year old girl. Unfortunately, her lifestyle made it almost impossible for her to be "normal."

"Are you going to help me today in science when we dissect our frog, Toby?" questioned Alyssa.

"Sure,... I guess,...... whatever! I'll see you later,..... I've got to get to class," whispered Toby as he shut his locker door reluctantly. He darted across the hall to room 123 where Reggie was awaiting impatiently.

"Toby, you were almost tardy again," scolded Reggie as they entered the classroom together. Toby couldn't help but notice the new boy to the right of him. He looked as though he was seventeen years old. His shoes were at least a size thirteen and by the looks of his legs he must have been at least six foot tall. Toby glanced over to Jordan and rolled his eyes toward the new boy.

"What's this kid's name?" Toby wrote quickly on a torn slip of paper. He folded the paper and slipped it gently into Reggie's notebook behind him.

"I don't know," whispered Reggie as he glanced over to Jeremiah. Jeremiah grabbed a piece of paper from his math book and began writing anxiously.

I saw you pointing to the new kid. His name is David Craig. He moved here from Louisville, Kentucky. His mom is the new principal at the high school. I heard he averaged 20 points a game last year in basketball. He'll be great for our team this year.

Jeremiah wadded the note and tossed it across the row to Toby. Toby made a diving catch as the note flew by his left ear and bounced off his desk onto the floor.

"Toby, please get out your assignment notebook!"

"Yes, Mr. Lee," Toby stuttered as he shoved the note into his shoe.

Mr. Lee was one of two seventh grade teachers. He was the youngest teacher at Sabens. His brown shoulder length hair and Lennon style focals accented his olive skin and blue eyes. His room supported learning centers with red oaken buckets of pencils, glue, scissors and other learning tools at each center. He only had one classroom rule posted on the front chalkboard that read........... RESPECT. Mr. Lee's allegiance to the Hoosiers was apparent through the numerous posters plastered on his classroom walls. Everyone looked forward to Mr. Lee's class.

"Today, class, we will be dissecting a frog, as we discussed yesterday. I have already placed a jar on each of your desks. Each jar contains the frog that will be your specimen."

"Will we be working with partners?" inquired Alyssa glancing across the room at Toby.

"Yes, Alyssa; however, I've already taken the liberty of pairing up the class."

"Toby, what if you have to work with her again?" shuttered Jordan.

Jordan was Toby's best friend. He had lived next door to Toby for eleven of his twelve years of life. They were on the same baseball, soccer, and basketball teams. Jordan was a good four inches taller than everyone else in the seventh grade. He never let sports come between their friendship. He was Toby's very best friend.

"Jordan, don't worry about me. I'm not going to do her work for her this time. She's got to learn to be more responsible," continued Toby.

"Toby, are we interrupting your conversation by having class?" Mr. Lee questioned sternly.

Everyone's eyes focused on Toby as he sank down in his seat in embarrassment. Realizing Alyssa's blue eyes were fixed on him, his cheeks turned a pale shade of red. Alyssa quickly glanced down at her notebook and began to write as though she had no idea what had just happened.

"Toby!"

"Yes, Mr. Lee," squeaked Toby in a high pitched voice.

"Are you ready?"

Everyone glared again at him waiting for his next response. Toby was known for his witty demeanor. He was charming, had a sense of humor, and could talk his way out of anything. Toby glanced across the room to Jordan and Jeremiah, but neither one of them acknowledged his presence.

"Sorry, Mr. Lee. I was just............"

"AHH!!!!!!!!!!!!!! My frog isn't breathing," cried Alyssa hysterically.

"Mine isn't either," laughed Reggie.

"Mine isn't either," said Jordan jokingly.

"That's enough, boys," Mr. Lee said impatiently with a wide grin on his face. "Alyssa, we have to put the frog asleep before we can dissect it," he continued.

"I can't believe you didn't know that, Alyssa," Toby replied rolling his green eyes from one side to the other.

"Let's continue, class," Mr. Lee charged, directing their attention to the large frog overhead image on the screen.

*"Would Toby Fields please report to the office,"* announced Ms. Foley over the intercom.

All eyes zoned on Toby.

"Toby, what did you do?" questioned Reggie softly.

"Nothing today," chuckled Toby. Toby

grabbed his books and strolled leisurely down to the office. He waved to Ms. Himes, the librarian, as he rounded the corner of the seventh grade hallway and past the music and art pod. As he maneuvered himself down the sixth grade hallway, he stopped to help Cindy Sauer, the counselor, carry a load of books to her office. When Toby reached the office Miss Foley stood at the doorway with her arms extended toward him. Her ashen colored face made Toby stop suddenly.

"What's wrong, Miss Foley?" trembled Toby.

"I just received a call from your mother and............"

# Chapter 2

"What?" interrupted Toby. "What's wrong with my mother?"

"It's not your mother, Toby, it's your dad. He's had an accident at home," shuddered Miss Foley.

Toby looked at Miss Foley in bewilderment. He could feel his heart palpitating through his blue hooded sweatshirt as his body began to quake uncontrollably.

"Where's my dad?" stuttered Toby as the tears streamed down his flushed face.

"Your dad is on his way to St. Nichol's Hospital. He fell down your basement stairs at home and hit his head on the concrete when he landed. The ambulance is there right now. Your Aunt Janice will be here in about five minutes to pick you up."

Toby stood speechless as though he had just seen a ghost. He tried to speak, but his mouth felt like he had just eaten a handful of cotton balls. Toby began to cry hysterically as thoughts of his dad raced through his head. Suddenly a tall, dark headed woman bolted through the front office doors.

"Aunt Janice," cried Toby, "you're here!"

"Let's go, Toby. Thank you, Miss Foley, for all of your help. We will be in touch later."

Jeremiah, Reggie, and Jordan peered through the classroom windows at their friend. They all stood with their mouths wide open as they watched their very best friend dart out the front doors of the school with tears streaming like waterfalls down his red cheeks. They knew something was very wrong.

Toby was speechless as they sped toward St. Nichol's Hospital. It was the longest ten minutes Toby had ever experienced. As they passed Austin Community Park, memories of his summer baseball games paralyzed his mind. His dad, Wayne, had been his little league coach for the last three years. Toby was very proud of his dad. He had been a minor league baseball player after college in Ohio. His 6'4" stature was perfect for a third baseman. His dad loved baseball and encouraged all of the boys to do their very best and have fun!

Toby stared blankly out the window of the blue pick-up truck as they passed Kay's Diner. The aroma of hamburgers and French fries engulfed the truck. Kay's Diner was one block from the park; it was the teams' after game hang-out. Toby's dad always treated the team to a round of cherry sodas and French fries after every game. He was the best dad a boy could have.

"Toby, we're here," Janice announced softly.

"I'm scared, Aunt Janice," Toby responded as they entered the emergency parking lot of the hospital.

"You have to be strong, Dear. Your mom needs you right now."

Janice clasped Toby's right hand and escorted him through the double glass doors of the emergency room. A noxious stench hit Toby in the face almost immediately. His stomach began to churn and sweat poured from his forehead. He had never been in a hospital before. Toby didn't see his dad anywhere. Where was he? Had he died? Suddenly a large brown-haired man appeared from behind a white tattered curtain.

"Are you Toby?" the man inquired extending his hand towards Toby.

"Yes," Toby stuttered softly. "Who are you?"

"I'm Dr. Richards. We've been waiting for you to get here. There's been an accident!"

Toby's heart was beating so fast it felt like it was jumping out of his shirt. His eyes were filled with tears, but he tried to hold them back. Every part of his body began to sweat and ache. His legs began to tremble; Toby fell to the ground as though his legs were suddenly paralyzed.

"Toby!" shrieked a woman from behind the curtain.

"Mom!" bawled Toby.

"Your dad fell down the basement steps after you left for school this morning. I was in the shower and didn't hear him fall."

Toby's mom spoke in a soft, but reassuring tone. She caressed Toby's back and held his left hand tightly to her side. Her brown eyes were swollen and blood-shot as she tried to fight back the tears that were streaming from within. Her long, red hair was still wet and thrown back into a pony tail. Laura Fields was the backbone of the family. She was a true optimist.

"Mrs. Fields," interrupted the doctor, "I need to talk to you privately."

"I'll stay here with Toby; we'll be fine," said

Janice reassuringly.

Dr. Richards escorted Toby's mom to the critical care waiting room. Mrs. Fields walked confidently down the yellow tiled hallway to the elevator. She held her head high as the elevator crept floor by floor until it reached the fifth floor. She could feel her heart dropping floor by floor. Dr. Richards stared blankly ahead holding fast to Mrs. Field's arm.

"We're here," whispered Dr. Richards graciously.

"Your husband has suffered a brain hematoma. We have been unable to slow the bleeding in his brain. We're doing everything we can. He's unconscious, but he is responding to stimulation."

"Can I see him?"

"Yes! Follow me."

Mrs. Fields sauntered slowly into room 501. The only sounds in the room were those of monitors humming, ringing, and buzzing almost in rhythm. Mrs. Fields stared aimlessly at the green and red lines racing across the monitors. Mr. Fields was tied up in tubes and bandages from head to foot. His head was as big as a watermelon with two eyes bulging through the mummy-like bandages. Looking down at her unrecognizable husband, she knew the next forty-eight hours would be crucial. She drew close to his side and immediately reached for his lifeless hand.

# Chapter 3

"Toby!" shouted Jordan.

"SHH! You're in a hospital," scolded Toby. "I'm glad you guys are here!"

"What happened?....... Ms. Foley told us your dad had an accident......... Is he going to be ok?" inquired Jeremiah excitedly.

"I don't know. I haven't seen him yet." Toby uttered reluctantly.

"Where's your mom?" asked Reggie.

"She's with the doctor. He wanted to talk to her alone. I'm sure she'll be back in a few minutes," Toby said confidently.

"We're going to stay here with you, Toby!" Jordan exclaimed proudly.

*"Would Toby and Janice Fields please report to*

*the information desk, please!"*

"Toby, that's you!" blurted Jordan.

"I'll call you guys later. Thanks for coming to see me."

"We're not leaving, Toby. We'll stay down here and watch television. We'll even miss school the rest of the day if we have to," Jeremiah reputed anxiously.

"Who brought you here?" questioned Toby curiously.

"Nobody! We walked here by ourselves. It was only about six blocks," Reggie said nonchalantly plopping down on the hospital lobby sofa.

"Does Ms. Foley know you're here?"

"Ah...........not really," stuttered Jeremiah.

"Toby, we have to go," interrupted Janice.

"I'll talk to you guys later!" Toby shouted as he exited the lobby.

Janice and Toby reported to the information desk next to the gift shop.

"Good morning! Our names were just paged. My name is Janice Fields."

"Yes, Maam. The doctor would like you to come up now. Mr. Fields is in room 501."

"Maybe we should get Dad a gift before we go up," Toby said enthusiastically.

"I think that's a great idea. What would you like to get him?" Janice asked as she pulled out her leather billfold from her knapsack.

Toby scanned the gift shop and spotted an autographed baseball in a collector's case. "This baseball is perfect! I know he'll love it!"

Toby grinned proudly and handed the ball to the cashier. The cashier wrapped the baseball carefully in red tissue paper and gently placed it inside a white gift bag.

"I know your dad will love this, too," echoed the cashier.

Janice and Toby thanked the cashier and began the journey to the fifth floor. The pattern of yellow tiles seemed endless. Finally, they reached the elevator that would take them to Toby's dad. The glass elevator traveled upward through the marbleized staircases and railings. Toby could see everything throughout the entire hospital as they ascended to the fifth floor. He clasped Janice's hand tightly as the elevator jolted to a halt.

Toby trembled anxiously when the elevator doors opened hesitantly. He peered into the corridor of the fifth floor and held the new baseball close to his chest. Ear piercing bells, alarms, and moans bombarded him like a fireworks display as he stepped from the elevator.

"Toby!" cried his mom.

"Mom, is Dad ok?.......... Where is he?........... Can I see him?"

"Toby," Janice interrupted, "let's take a walk down to the waiting room with your mom."

"Thank you, Janice."

"Everything will be fine, Laura. I called Jim;

he's on his way."

"Wayne's still unconscious. I don't know if he'll even know if his own brother is in the room."

Laura buried her worn face into her hands as she leaned on Toby for support. Being the only child, Toby knew that it was up to him to take care of his mom. He draped her tangled red hair over her left shoulder and tucked a pillow gently behind her lower back as they sat together on the red leather couch.

As Toby sensitively caressed his mom's shoulders, he spotted two other people across the room. A large, robust man was staring blankly out the octagon shaped stained glass window onto the terrace of the hospital lawn. His left hand was interlocked tightly with a young woman twenty years his younger. The young woman with her head held high, legs crossed lifelessly, and hands cupped securely across her linen skirt, caught a glimpse of Toby as he stared curiously at her. The woman smiled reassuringly at Toby like a mother does toward her baby. Toby returned the smile and, without a thought, kissed his mom gently on the cheek.

"Mrs. Fields,...........Mrs. Fields," Dr. Richards echoed softly.

"Is he done? Can I see him?"

"Done, done with what?" Toby questioned insistently.

"Your dad had a CT Scan on his head," his mother said pointedly.

"What is a CT Scan?"

Dr. Richards interjected, "A CT Scan is like an X-ray. It provides a detailed image of your dad's brain."

"Does it hurt?" asked Toby as he scratched his head.

"No! It's a very simple and painless procedure. Your dad had to lay flat on his back on a movable table. The table was then guided to the center of the scanner that looked like a gigantic doughnut............. Would you like to see him?"

"Can I, Mom?"

Toby wiped his eyes, tucked in his wrinkled shirt, and tied his left shoe.

"Do I look ok, Mom?"

Toby's mom gazed at him with a sparkle in her eye and replied, "Your dad is very proud of you."

Toby took a deep breath and followed the doctor out of the waiting room. Janice proceeded close behind escorting Toby's mom.

"Here we are, room 501," whispered Dr. Richards.

Toby peered cautiously into the darkened room. Inside the door to the right was a brown leather chair draped with the day's newspaper. Above the chair was a television suspended from the ceiling. Toby glanced to his left and spied his dad, seeing first the white head turban.

"What's wrong with Dad's head?...... It's so big!" shouted Toby in shock.

"SHH!! His head is swollen from the fall. It'll go back down eventually," his mom uttered softly.

"But, Mom, his head is bigger than a watermelon. I can't even see his eyes...... Can he still see?........... AHH!! What's that sound? ............What's wrong, Mom?" Toby panicked and threw his arms around his mother's neck.

"It's a call alarm for the nurse, Toby. Everything's ok! ............ See that bag hanging above your dad's head?"

"Yes........"

"That bag holds your dad's medicine. When the bag is empty, an alarm sounds to let the nurse know that it's time to refill it."

"Hello, Mrs. Fields. It looks like it's time to change bags again."

Toby watched the nurse carefully as she

removed the empty bag from the tall aluminum pole that was plotted next to his dad's bed. The pole had a long sharp arm like a pirate's hook for the bag to hang on.

"Who's this nice looking young man standing beside you?"

"This is my son Toby."

"Glad to meet you, Toby. I'm sure I'll be seeing a lot of you."

Toby smiled and shrugged his shoulders as he glanced up at his mom's face to see her response.

"Mom, can I talk to Dad alone?"

Mrs. Fields hesitated as she wiped a stray tear from Toby's flushed face.

"I'll wait outside with Aunt Janice."

Toby pulled up the brown leather chair to the side of the bed and grasped his dad's right hand tightly. His hand was warm and clammy against Toby's palm. Toby studied the array of tubing extruding from his dad's body. There were small clear tubes attached to his left hand, tubes stuck in his nose, and a large balloon like tube was lodged in his mouth and taped securely.

"Dad, if you can hear me, squeeze my hand."

Toby waited for a response....................but nothing.

"Dad, I never thanked you for the new basketball you bought me last Saturday...... It's a great basketball......... Everyone wants to borrow it at recess."

Toby paused briefly.

"I got a B+ on my math test yesterday......... Mrs. Anderson says I've really improved this second six weeks of school.......... I told her you had been helping me with my fractions............. I bragged a little and told her how smart you are."

Toby drew his chair closer to the bed and tucked the blanket securely around his dad's shoulders.

"We start basketball practice next Monday. I

think this year is going to be my year. Jeremiah thinks I have a good chance of making starting guard. I've been working on my left-hand lay-ups............. The advice you gave me has really helped...................... I'll work harder this year, Dad, I promise!"

Toby waited patiently for his dad to answer or squeeze his hand. His mind became overwrought with images of his dad laying in the hospital bed forever. What if he never came home? What if he could never talk again? What if?............... Toby blocked the thought of death from his mind. Tears began to swell in his eyes once again with the idea of losing his dad.

"Toby?" inquired a low quirky voice.

Toby jerked to the right and glared over his right shoulder. A tall, thin shadow graced the archway of the room.

"Uncle Jim, you're here!" exclaimed Toby.

Toby jumped up from the chair, with a grin

as wide as a carved pumpkin, and embraced his uncle tightly.

"How's your dad, Toby?"

Toby couldn't respond.

"I'm sorry it took me so long to get here."

"I'm glad you're here, Uncle Jim," Toby stuttered softly.

"Why don't you go with your mom and get some dinner down in the cafeteria. You've had a long afternoon. I'll meet you down stairs shortly."

"Ok, Uncle Jim."

Toby held his head high and strutted out of his dad's room. He spotted his mom pacing the hallway just steps from his dad's room. She had been pacing for fifteen minutes back and forth between rooms 501 and 515. Her black mascara was smudged across her flushed cheeks and her tangled hair was flowing freely down her back. Once into the hallway, Toby lowered his head and bolted into his mom's arms.

"Mom, he couldn't even hear me!" cried Toby.

Toby quickly wiped his tears and jumped back from his mom's arms.

"Did he see me?" questioned Toby cautiously.

"Did who see you?" replied his mom.

"Uncle Jim! I don't want him to see me cry."

Toby's mom clasped Toby's hands tightly and replied with a slight stutter, "It's ok if you cry, Toby."

"Uncle Jim said that real men don't cry. I don't want to disappoint him," Toby explained.

"Would you like to get some dinner? You have some visitors downstairs waiting for you," his mom interjected.

"I do? Who's here?" questioned Toby excitedly.

"You'll see," smiled his mom.

"Let's take the stairs," suggested Toby. "I need my exercise."

Toby and his mom descended down the five floors silently. They both stared ahead floor by floor, hand in hand.

"Hey, Toby!" echoed a chorus from the bottom of the stairs.

"Hey, guys! I thought you went home a long time ago."

"We just got here. We've been talking to your Aunt Janice for awhile," replied Jeremiah. "Your mom called our parents; they said we could stay here and have dinner with you."

"Thanks, guys!" exclaimed Toby. "Let's get some dinner; I'm starving."

The four boys followed the yellow tiles toward the cafeteria. Janice and Mrs. Fields trailed them close behind.

"Laura, what is the doctor's prognosis?" questioned Janice.

Laura stopped in her tracks and looked at Janice grimly.

"Dr. Richards said he will be here for at least

six weeks," Laura stated bluntly.

Both women were silent as the tears streamed down their faces like running water from a faucet. They clasped one another's hand and walked speechlessly toward the cafeteria.

# Chapter 4

The sun rays warmed Toby's face as they penetrated his bedroom window. Toby rolled over and pulled his bedspread tightly over his head. The aroma of pancakes and sausage engulfed his room as his alarm sounded with a loud chiming echo. He threw his bedspread off the bed and jumped to his feet. With two giant leaps, he sprung into the hallway and headed towards the bathroom. The house was quiet; only the crackling of sausage in the frying pan could be heard. Toby tiptoed down the hallway past his mother and dad's room.

"Mom!" gasped Toby with a surprised look on his face. "Why are you packing a suitcase?"

"Toby, we need to talk. Come in here and sit down."

"Are you leaving, too?" Toby asked with a puzzled look on his face. He sauntered cautiously towards his mother and sat down next to her on the bed. Toby looked his mom in the eyes and could see that this was going to be a serious conversation. He had seen this look before......................... Toby gazed out the window and thought back to the previous summer. He would never forget their last Fourth of July party; if only he had listened to Jeremiah and Reggie. Toby remembered the look in his mom's eyes as she apologized to the neighbors for his bad choices. At the time, he didn't think firecrackers could do so much damage to a mailbox. It wasn't only the look that Toby remembered, but what his mom had said. Toby cringed as he thought back to those dreadful words his mother had spoken to him................

....................

*"I guess I can't trust you anymore, Toby."*

Shivers raced throughout Toby's body as the

memories of Fourth of July haunted him once more.

"Toby, what are you thinking about?"

"Nothing, Mom. What did you want to talk to me about?" He wiped the sweat from his forehead with his pajama sleeve and tucked the bed pillow deep into his chest.

"I'm going to be staying with your dad at the hospital for awhile. Dr. Richards said that your dad is going to be there for several more weeks."

"What about me? Who's going to stay with me?" Toby blurted out throwing the pillow to the floor. Toby bounded from the bed and hurdled the ottoman as he sped toward the bedroom door.

"Toby, wait!" cried his mom as she dashed towards the door behind Toby.

Toby stopped abruptly and turned towards his mom.

"I'm sorry, Mom," he cried as he threw his arms around her neck.

"I love you, Toby!"

"I love you, too!" Toby echoed as he held his mother tightly. "What's that smell?"

"Oh, no! My sausage!"

Toby darted out of the bedroom and flew down the railing of the staircase. Smoke grazed his eyes coupled with the smell of torched sausage as he slid barefooted into the white tiled kitchen.

"Mom, hurry!" choked Toby. "Where's that fire extinguisher?" Toby peered through the smoke filled room as if opening curtains with his hands.

"There it is!" Toby screamed. He grabbed the extinguisher from the wall behind the sink and ripped off the medal secure tab and began spraying white foam sporadically around the kitchen.

"Toby, are you ok?" Mrs. Fields cried as she watched Toby in amazement from the kitchen doorway.

"Everything's under control, Mom!" Toby said proudly while spewing the last bit of foam from the extinguisher. "I think I sprayed your sausage, too!"

"That's ok, Toby!............ Are you ok?................ .......... I'm very proud of you!" his mom exclaimed as she grabbed the frying pan and threw it into the sink. "Help me open the windows. Let's get some of this smoke out of here."

The smoke began to dissipate quickly. Toby helped his mom wipe up the counter and discard the blistered sausage.

"I didn't hear the smoke detector. Did you!" questioned Toby.

"With all of the commotion, I really didn't pay attention. But I think you're right."

"I'll get it checked out, Mom!" Toby said calmly as he climbed carefully onto the kitchen chair and reached for the smoke detector above the vaulted doorway.

"We'll have your Uncle Jim take a look when he gets here. Get down from the chair before you hurt yourself."

"I can do it, Mom," Toby responded persistently. Toby pulled the cover from the alarm and yanked out the batteries. He jumped from the chair and scurried to the kitchen "grab" drawer.

"What are you looking for?"

"The battery tester is in this drawer somewhere. Dad always uses it to check the batteries," Toby replied confidently.

Toby's mom smiled proudly as she watched him replace the dead batteries in the smoke detector and install the unit securely back onto the wall.

"Toby, I'll clean up down here. You go on upstairs and get dressed for school."

"I'll help, Mom!" Toby said anxiously while wiping the counters with a wet rag.

"We have a long day ahead of us, Toby. Go upstairs and get dressed and I'll finish up." Mrs. Fields paused for a moment then turned to Toby, clasped his hands in hers and said, "You're growing up!"

Toby blushed, hugged his mom, and ran for the stairs. He darted up the stairs and paused at the top of the landing.

"Mom!" Toby shouted as he leaned over the staircase.

"Yes, Dear!"

"Did you say get dressed for school?"

"Yes, I did!"

Toby leaped down the flight of stairs in a panic.

"But, Mom," pleaded Toby, "I thought I was going to the hospital with you?"

"I've already talked to your principal, Ms. Foley. I explained what happened to your dad and that you might be missing some school. I think you should go today and take your mind off of things. I'll call the school if there are any changes. Now, go upstairs and get ready for school. I'll drop you off on my way to the hospital."

# Chapter 5

"Toby!" screamed Reggie from the basketball courts next to the parking lot.

"Hey, Reggie," responded Toby as he tipped his baseball cap toward the crowd of students gathered around center court. He jogged out to the courts and greeted his friends with high fives and belly smacks.

"Good thing you're back today!" exclaimed Jordan.

"Yeah," echoed Reggie and Jeremiah.

"Why's that? ...... What's going on today?"

"Remember, ..today we're dissecting mice in Mr. Lee's class!" Jordan wailed excitedly.

"Sweet!..........I love that class!" Toby responded as he strutted towards the front doors of the school.

"Maybe we can be lab partners, Jordan!.... Mr. Lee usually sticks me with a girl..........Hey, how did practice go last night?"

"Ahhhh....fine...I guess...," stuttered Reggie.

"What do you mean by that?"

"Nothing. I just mean it went ok. Don't worry about it; you'll be fine."

Toby's face turned two shades of red as his jaw tightened. He stared into Reggie's eyes as he butted up against his chest and said, "Don't worry about what?"

Suddenly a sweet flowery scent captured Toby's attention. Toby jerked his head to the left; there stood Alyssa. She flipped her red backpack over her shoulder and tossed Toby a quick wink as she sauntered by his locker. Toby grinned, the sweat trickling down his forehead and the back of his neck.

"Toby, ..Toby!" interrupted Reggie. "Let's get to class before we get another tardy."

"I've only had three tardies this six weeks. Besides, Ms. Foley likes me," responded Toby proudly.

"Hey, I'll catch you later. Good luck tonight!" responded Reggie.

"Good luck tonight with what?........... What are you talking about?......... Is there something going on with basketball I don't know about?"

"Toby, the teams are going to be posted after school... I told you earlier you'd be fine.... No need to worry... Everybody knows you've been under a little stress with your dad and all," Reggie said reassuringly as he patted Toby on the shoulder.

"What if I don't make the "A" team?"

"You'll be fine!"

"But, what if I don't? My dad will be so disappointed!"

"Toby, you'll be fine!.........................Oh great, there went the tardy bell. I've got to go, I'll see you later."

The four boys watched the clock tick idly period by period. Finally, three o'clock approached and the final bell wailed for the day to end. A stream of boys dashed to the gym hall bulletin board like bulls out of a pen. The dreaded list had been posted. The boys hovered around the list like hawks around their prey.

"Hey, Jordan, should we wait for Jeremiah and Toby to get here before we look?"

"Yeah! We better wait for them," Jordan said with a puzzled look, standing behind the crowd of boys perched at the bulletin board.

Jordan and Reggie meandered their way through the thinning crowd towards the basketball bulletin board.

"Do you see them yet?"

"No!"

"Where are they? I told Toby to meet me here after school."

"Here they come!" responded Jordan.

"Have you guys looked at the list yet?" inquired Jeremiah.

"No, we were waiting for you guys to get here."

"I can't look. My dad will be so mad if I don't make it!" Toby replied.

"My dad will really be upset if I don't make it," echoed Jeremiah.

"Ok, who's going to look? Jordan, you look."

"Why do I have to look, Toby?"

"Because we all know you'll be on the list! You're the best one!"....................

The four boys made their move towards the list. Jordan positioned his index finger at the top of the list and began his descent down the page name by name.

"Toby, you made the team. Your name is on the list!" exclaimed Jordan.

"Are you sure? I can't believe I made it! Who else is on the list?"

Toby joined Jordan in examining the list of names.

"Look, Jared made the team. So did Erik," responded Jordan.

"Hey, look! David, the new kid, made it! He'll be great for the team. He's really good!" exclaimed Jeremiah.

"Jordan, where's your name?............ It has to be on there............ You're our best player!" Toby said reassuringly.

"Hey, Reggie,...Jeremiah,....you're in!" shouted Toby.

"What about me?" questioned Jordan enthusiastically.

Toby and the boys scanned the list one more time, name by name.

"Ah................here's your name. You're on the team, Jordan!" announced Jeremiah.

After a round of high-fives, the four boys threw their gym bags and backpacks over their shoulders and strutted down the hallway towards the locker room. Toby's grin was suddenly sabotaged as he turned the corner by the athletic office and saw David talking to Alyssa next to the girls' locker room doors. Toby nudged Jeremiah in the side and whispered sarcastically, "Why isn't David in the locker room getting ready?........... Why is he talking to Alyssa?.............Let's turn around and go back the other way."

"That will look too obvious. Let's just keep going, Toby. They probably won't even say anything."

"Hi, Toby!" Alyssa said in a whimsical high pitched voice.

"Oh, hi, Alyssa."

"How's your dad?"

Toby's face reddened like the coals on a fire. He stared at Alyssa and David as he struggled to spit out a reply. Toby turned suddenly and dashed down the hallway and out the west doors next to the football field.

"Way to go, Alyssa," blurted Jeremiah angrily. "Why did you have to ask him about his dad? He's still in the hospital. Toby only gets to see him for fifteen minutes today after practice."

"Jeremiah, relax. Alyssa was trying to be nice. We all care about Toby's dad," responded David. "Is there anything the team can do for him?"

Jeremiah cocked his head to the left and then to the right and peered suspiciously down the hallway. He pulled David close to his chest by grabbing the sleeve of his t-shirt and whispered subtly, "We can let him be the star of our first game Thursday night."

David shook Jeremiah's hand, using the team's secret handshake, and followed Jeremiah out the front door, both with grins as wide as a crescent moon.

# Chapter 6

Toby vaulted from the bus and skittered hurriedly to his Aunt's house. He could hardly wait to see his dad. He jumped up onto the front deck and bolted into the house like a streak of lightening. Toby announced enthusiastically, "I'm home Aunt Janice." His voice vibrated up through the cherry spiral staircase. "Hello!" Toby repeated. Silence permeated throughout the house as Toby peered around the dining room accordion doors. Toby thrashed through the doors into the kitchen where he spied a plate of freshly baked peanut butter cookies. Toby grabbed a cookie and inhaled it. He continued to grab three more cookies until the plate was half empty. Toby realized he was home alone! Where was Aunt Janice?

"Who's here?" shouted Toby as the front door squeaked open slowly. Toby jumped up from the bar stool and popped his head around the corner of the dining room. "Who's here?" repeated Toby. Shivers spilled down his back. He jerked his neck suddenly to the right and caught a glimpse of a gray image scurrying towards the kitchen door. Toby lunged towards the door and exclaimed, "Johnny, you scared me! What are you doing inside? How did you get in?"

"Toby, where are you?"

"Aunt Janice, is that you?"

As Toby twisted to his left a cold hand stroked his shoulder. "Aunt Janice, where have you been? It's 5:30. I was supposed to meet you here at 5:00 so that I could go see Dad."

"I've been to the hospital; there's been a change in your dad's condition."

"Change?.... What change?............ Mom was supposed to call me at school if something was wrong."

"Your mom didn't want to worry you."

"Is Dad ok?"

"Get your clothes changed, Toby. We need to meet your mom at the hospital right away!"

Toby scurried into the bathroom and changed out of his basketball warm-ups and wiped a cold, wet rag across his forehead and down the back of his neck. His heart began fluttering as he stuffed his clothes back in his bag.

"I'm ready, Aunt Janice. Let's hurry!"

Janice and Toby jumped into the truck and raced to the hospital without uttering a sound between them.

"Where's Mom?" Toby asked breaking the silence.

"She's waiting for us at the information desk. We should be there in a couple of minutes."

Toby jumped out of the truck and tore off for the front doors of the hospital as Janice made a screeching stop in the emergency parking lot.

"Mom!" shouted Toby embracing her tightly inside the front lobby.

"Toby, they just took your dad to surgery!"

"Surgery! What's going on! Why didn't you call me at school?"

"Your dad took a turn for the worse just a short time ago. Janice went to the school to pick you up from practice, but you had already left."

"What happened?" choked Toby.

"All I know is your dad's head is filling up with fluid. They have to drain it in order to control the swelling. They've taken him to the third floor for emergency surgery."

Toby could see the distress in his mom's eyes. He clasped her left hand tightly and embedded his head into her shoulder for comfort. Toby could feel her heart palpitating in rhythm with his own. He held tight to his mom as tears began dripping down his face onto his collar.

Darkness soon settled on the waiting room. Toby's head bobbed left to right as he fought to stay awake. Time seemed to stand still. Mrs. Fields began pacing the floor in an effort to calm her nerves. Toby glanced frequently at the large, black faced clock tick effortlessly throughout the night as he cradled his basketball under his left arm.

"Mrs. Fields!.....Mrs. Fields!....wake up!" nudged Dr. Richards.

"Mom!" shouted Toby, "wake up!"

"I have good news!" exclaimed the doctor. "Your husband has made it through the surgery. We were able to suppress the blood and fluid drainage successfully. Would you like to see him?"

"Is he awake?"

"He's semi-conscious right now. He can hear you, but he might not be able to respond."

"Mom, can I go, too?"

"Is it ok, Dr. Richards?"

"Certainly, I'm sure your dad will be glad to see you. Come with me."

Toby and his mom followed the doctor down the hallway to the elevator. Taking the familiar trip down the yellow-tiled hallway was becoming a habit for Toby and his mom.

"This isn't the same floor as last time is it?" questioned Toby.

"Good observation, Toby. We're actually going to the third floor, the surgical floor. Your dad is in the recovery room. He'll be in this room the rest of the night so that we can keep a close eye on him."

Toby and his mom stepped off the elevator and followed the doctor down the hallway to the recovery room.

"Mom, it's cold in here."

"It is cold in here," replied Toby's mom.

"Look at all of these machines hooked up to dad," whispered Toby as he approached his dad's bedside.

Mrs. Fields clasped her husband's clammy hands beneath the blankets and sat gently on the side of the bed, careful not to disturb him. "Toby, come over here and sit next to me. We will hold your dad's hands together."

Toby crept around the bed and sat next to his mom like a small bear cub. Toby held his dad's hands tightly and caressed his forehead while his mom tucked the blankets tightly around his shoulders. They both sat quietly listening to the rhythm of the heart monitor as Toby's dad lay motionless.

# Chapter 7

"Where's Toby?" shouted Reggie as he sprinted down the hallway towards science class.

"Why isn't he at his locker?" echoed Jeremiah trailing Reggie.

"I didn't see him during first hour. Did you?" questioned Reggie.

"Something's not right. Toby wouldn't miss our first basketball game unless something was really wrong. He's got to be here tonight for the game. It's his big chance."

"I know. This doesn't make sense. Where is he?"

"Do you think something happened to his dad last night?" questioned Jeremiah.

Reggie and Jeremiah paused and peered down

the hallway before opening the door to science class. No Toby in sight. The boys slipped into class and took their respective seats without notice.

"Class, today we will be discussing the water cycle. Can anyone tell me where water begins?"

"How can we discuss the water cycle at a time like this," interrupted Jordan.

"At a time like what?" replied Mr. Lee.

"Toby! Toby isn't here today. It's our first game and he's not here," shouted Jeremiah.

"I'm sure Toby is ok!" assured Mr. Lee.

"What if something happened to his dad last night?" inquired Alyssa.

Mr. Lee stared silently at Toby's empty desk as the class sat solemnly peering out the window to the front courtyard. "Why don't we have a silent reading session today on the water cycle. We will plan to discuss the chapter tomorrow," he uttered in a low shaky voice.

"Maybe we should call Toby's house," suggested

Reggie.

"You'd think he'd at least text us if something was going on," echoed Jeremiah.

Mr. Lee interrupted, "Boys, I'm sure if something was wrong, Toby would have called one of you. He probably overslept. Let's get back to the reading."

The boys watched the clock approach 11:00 a.m. as they sauntered down the hallway to the cafeteria.

"You'd think they would do away with broccoli at school. Nobody eats broccoli," uttered Reggie as the boys spooled their way through the lunch line.

"I know, even my clothes end up smelling like that stuff," replied Jordan.

"This has sure been a long morning."

"I know, Jeremiah, I don't know how I can eat at a time like this," replied Reggie.

"I don't even feel like eating," said Jeremiah

sluggishly trying to balance his spoon on his nose.

"I know the feeling," responded Jordan.

"Toby!!!" screamed Jeremiah.

Silence settled over the cafeteria…………… Suddenly a loud cheer plagued the entire room.

"It's Toby!" exclaimed Alyssa.

"Toby, buddy, where have you been?…….. Is your dad ok?………….. Is everything alright?"

Toby stood numb as his friends gathered around him like hawks around their prey.

"Hey!" muttered Toby. "I'm starving! What's for lunch?"

"It's your favorite, Toby! Chicken and noodles!" exclaimed Reggie, "and broccoli."

"Let's eat!" Toby shouted as he sprinted towards the food line.

The boys gathered together at their table and began planning their strategy for the big game as they inhaled several helpings of chicken and noodles.

"How many days have you double-trayed, Jeremiah?"

"This is my tenth day in a row. There's no way I can get by with one tray."

"Toby, how's your dad?" interrupted Alyssa.

Toby stopped the shoveling process momentarily and responded, "He had emergency surgery last night.................I stayed most of the night with him............I'll know later today if he's going to make it."

"If he's going to make it?" questioned Jordan. "What do you mean? Is he going to die?"

"He might," Toby responded sheepishly.

"Toby," interrupted Ms. Foley approaching the boy's table. "I just heard the news. Is there anything I can do?"

"No, Ms. Foley, I'm ok. I'm glad I'm here with my friends."

"Your mom said she would call if there were

any changes."

"Are you going to play tonight, Toby?" charged Jeremiah.

"I wouldn't miss it!" Toby grinned proudly.

# Chapter 8

The first game of the season was finally here. Toby's hands trembled as he watched the clock tick hour by hour until 3:00. Jeremiah, Reggie, Jordan, and Toby sped toward the locker room at the sound of the 3:05 bell. The locker room was consumed with excitement and enthusiasm. The team gathered as Coach Jensen summoned the boys into a huddle. The boys listened attentively to Coach Jensen's game plan. The horn sounded as the boys ran onto the court for the tip-off. Toby looked to the stands for his mom, even though he knew she wasn't there.

The referee threw the ball and David controlled the tip to Jordan in the back court. Jordan dribbled the ball down the floor and hit David for the lay-up.

"Way to get the game started," hollered Coach Jensen from the bench.

The Cougar's guard answered by running down the length of the court for the shot through all five Star's players.

"Boys, defense! Watch your man!"

The quarter ended with David lighting it up behind the arch. Toby waited patiently on the bench for his time to shine as he watched his team crush the Cougars by ten points at the end of the first quarter.

"Good first quarter, boys. Keep up the good work. Let's go into a zone during the second quarter."

The Cougars turned it around in the second quarter scoring six unanswered points. "Time-out," bellowed Coach Jensen with only three minutes left in the half.

"We need to relax out there. Boys, stay with

your man. We're missing the guy underneath every time. Now on three, TEAM!"

As the boys took the floor, Coach Jensen skewed the bench for a substitute to replace Jeremiah as forward. Toby perked up and started for the floor as the coach pointed to Eric. Toby dropped his shoulders and sat back down with a look of disappointment. The first half came to a close with the Cougars on top by one.

The third quarter began with David hitting a three-point shot from the corner. The crowd screamed with excitement as the new star of Sabens continued to lead his team. During the Star's next possession, Reggie made a great dish to Jeremiah under the basket. Throughout the quarter David couldn't miss from long range. The third quarter ended with the Stars up by five.

"Good job, David; good effort out there. Boys, let's see six minutes of toughness out there. On three, TEAM!"

The fourth quarter started with the Cougar's star forward scoring seven straight points. The Stars answered back quickly with David's fifteen foot jumper. During the Star's next possession, Jordan passed the ball to Jared on the low block, but when he made his move he got called for his fifth foul. On the sidelines, Coach Jensen called Toby from the bench.

"Toby, since Jared fouled out, the team needs you to come through," charged the coach.

As Toby vaulted from the bench to the floor, he thought of his dad in the hospital. He knew his dad would be proud of him right now. Suddenly from the corner of his eye, he spied a woman standing at half-court waving frantically.

"Coach, my mom is here. Something is wrong!"

Toby instinctively dashed across the court to his mom.

"Mom, what's wrong?"

"Nothing, Toby. I'm here to watch your first

game."

"What about Dad?"

"Your dad woke up about two hours ago. He's going to be ok!"

Toby's eyes swelled with tears as he threw his arms around his mom and kissed her gently on the cheek.

"Go out there and play ball, Toby!" exclaimed his mom.

"Coach!" Toby screamed across the court, "he's ok.......my dad is ok!"

Coach Jensen called another time out and huddled the team together.

"Boys, let's do this for Toby's dad!"

"This is for Toby's dad!" repeated David.

"Let's finish this!" shouted Jordan.

With two minutes to go, the Cougars controlled the lead by two points. The clock continued to tick. David received the pass from Eric and dribbled down the court for the tie.

The Cougars and Stars were tied at 40 with 30 seconds to go in the game. The Cougar's guard came down the court with Toby guarding him. He pulled up for the shot and Toby made the mistake of fouling him. He went to the line with fifteen seconds to go. The Cougar player missed the first shot but made the second to put the Cougars up by one point. Coach Jensen called a time-out.

"David, I want you to take the final shot! Boys, whatever you do, get the ball to David! Ok, let's go! TEAM!"

The team put their hands in the middle and chanted, "Win!, Go Stars!! Win!" Toby passed the ball in to Reggie, and he dribbled down the court. David came off the screen but his defender fought his way through Eric's screen and wasn't open.

"Reggie, get the ball over to Jordan!" screeched Jeremiah from the bench.

Over on the sideline, Toby was five feet away from the basket, wide-open. Reggie threw the ball to Toby with three seconds still on the clock. Toby looked at the rim and fired up the shot, which went well past the basket. Toby sank his head as he realized he had just lost the game for the team.

Toby wrapped his hands over his ears and knelt to the ground. The buzz of defeat echoed throughout the gym. Toby's heart raced as though he had just run the marathon. He poked his head from underneath his arms and skewed the gym for familiar faces. The crowd mauled its way out the doors in disbelief. Toby stood to his feet, with his head hung and began walking toward the locker room. Jeremiah stood next to the door with his shoulders cocked back and the basketball tucked under his arm.

"Good game, Toby. You tried your best. It was a difficult shot."

"Thanks, Jeremiah. I'll see you tomorrow," choked Toby.

Jeremiah gave Toby a quick slap to the shoulder and left the locker room. Jordan and Reggie peered over the top of the shower lavatory as Toby shoved his uniform into his gym bag, slammed the locker door shut, and left the locker room.

"Mom, don't say anything...........I'm not in a very good mood right now," Toby scolded as he walked onto the court from the locker room.

"Toby, you gave it your best shot. That's all anyone can ask. I'm very proud of you and I know your dad would be very proud of you as well if he were here."

"I can't believe I lost the game."

"Toby, one person does not win nor lose a game..........It's a team effort!"

"Mom, please, I missed the winning basket!.........I need a few minutes, I'll meet you outside.

Toby sat with his elbows perched on his knees with his hands draped over his head as he replayed the final shot in his head over and over.

*"I can't believe I missed that shot...... It's my bread and butter shot........ I've never been able to hit buzzer shots......... Why did they give me the ball anyway? .......David should have taken the shot......I don't even like basketball.........I'm glad Dad wasn't here!!"*

# Chapter 9

"Mom!"

"Yes, Toby."

"When is Dad coming home?"

"Do you want another pancake? You have time for one more before school."

"Sure, I'll have another one; but, Mom, when is Dad coming home?" Toby questioned again while drowning his pile of pancakes with warm syrup.

Mrs. Fields dropped another teaspoon of mocha flavored creamer in her coffee as she flipped the final two cakes on the griddle.

"The doctor called this morning while you were in the shower. They've moved him back to the fifth floor.

"Why? What's wrong? I thought he was

getting better............ Is he dying?"

"The doctor said your dad might not be able to come home until Thanksgiving."

"Thanksgiving! That's a month away!" shouted Toby shoving his chair back from the table.

Toby threw down his fork, grabbed his backpack from the counter, and catapulted out the back door.

"Toby, wait!" ........................................

........................................

*"I don't understand. I thought Dad was ok! He's going to miss my whole basketball season,"* Toby mumbled to himself as he approached the bus stop.

"Toby,...Toby,........what's up?" uttered Reggie as he stepped onto the bus.

"Uh?"

"Toby, did you hear me?" repeated Reggie.

"Oh, hey, Reggie."

"Is something wrong? You look horrible!"

Toby paraded to the back seat followed by Reggie.

"Hey, Toby!" whispered Alyssa as she tugged on his sweatshirt.

"Hey, Alyssa!"

"What's up, Toby?" echoed David.

"Hey!"

"Toby, what's wrong with you today? You seem a little out of it," questioned Reggie.

"Well.............my mom just told me that Dad will be in the hospital until Thanksgiving!"

"You're kidding! That means he's going to miss all of your games."

"I know!"

"What about your dad, Reggie? Is he coming to our game Thursday? It's going to be a big game. The Buffaloes are the best team in the conference."

"Ah.......probably not. He works a lot," shrugged Reggie taking his cell phone from his backpack.

"It doesn't seem like he ever comes to the games. I thought your dad loved basketball? Didn't he play in high school?"

"Yeah! He sort of played. He always tells everyone this story about how he missed out on being a big star because of some kid named Jerry who moved to town in 7th grade. Dad pretty much sat the bench most of the time. He still talks about it a lot. I think it really bothers him that he never got a chance to play varsity."

"Why doesn't he come to our games?"

"It's just hard for him to make it with his work schedule, I guess," Reggie continued as he switched into game mode.

"How do you think we'll do Thursday?" questioned Toby.

"I don't know. It'll be tough. The Buffaloes are really good. They always seem to win the conference."

"I'm not sure I even want to play after our game last night."

"Toby, it was a good shot. You had to take it."

"I wish someone else would've taken the last shot. I never make those clutch shots."

"I don't mean to change the subject, but are you going to the hospital tonight after practice?"

"Yeah! They're moving Dad back to the fifth floor today."

"The fifth floor sounds kind of creepy. What's there?.......... Why does your dad always have to go back to that floor?"

"I'm not really sure........... I know there are a lot of nurses walking around...........and there are a lot of loud machines on the floor."

"What kind of machines?"

"You know.....just a lot of things people are hooked up to. There are lots of buzzers and bells going off all of the time. It is kind of creepy, I guess."

"Can your dad have visitors yet?"

"Well..........he doesn't really open his eyes much.... and his head is still covered in bandages. I can only see him for a little while.......... You guys probably shouldn't see him yet," stuttered Toby as the bus came to a sudden halt.

"What was that sound?" shouted David from the middle row of seats.

"Why are we stopped?" demanded Alyssa.

"Look, Toby!" exclaimed Reggie.

"Awesome!" gleamed Jeremiah.

Toby peered out the window to his left.

"Why are you grinning, Toby?" questioned Alyssa sitting on the edge of her seat like a queen on her throne.

"Well...it looks like we're going to be late for school," replied Toby as he propped his legs up on the seat.

"How can you relax at a time like this, Toby?"

Alyssa scolded making her way towards the front of the bus.

"At a time like this..........this is great. I'm going to miss my math test," Toby smirked under his breath.

"Alyssa gets way too worked up; she needs to relax," responded Reggie.

"I know."

"Attention...... everyone! Attention!..............
...........Quiet!!!"

"I wonder what Mr. Bennett wants?" questioned Jeremiah.

"Unfortunately, as you can see, we've run into a little problem. It's going to be at least another fifteen minutes before they can get the road totally cleared. They're sending another bus to pick you up."

"Pick us up. What's with that?" Reggie spouted out as he tore his headphones off.

"We'll still miss most of first hour..... Besides,

how cool is this?......... Mr. Jacobs' cows always get out, but I've never seen the whole herd cross the road at the same time. There must be a thousand of them........ This is awesome!...... It's going to take forever to get them all back in their own field. This day is definitely getting better! Nothing can spoil it now!"

"Look, the other bus is already here," pointed Reggie.

"Why's it here already? I was just getting relaxed........... I thought Mr. Bennett said it would be at least fifteen minutes..................... .................................. Great, now we're going to be on time!" muttered Toby.

"Hey! Sorry about the game last night, Toby. You almost made it. I was cheering for you!"

"Thanks, Alyssa, for bringing it up," interrupted Jeremiah.

"Yeah, can't you see Toby is still upset about it?" chimed Reggie.

"Thanks, Alyssa, but I'm trying to forget about it," Toby countered while stepping off the bus.

"Yeah, Alyssa, he's trying to forget about it..... You're making it worse!" shouted Jordan as he patted Toby on the back.

"Let's go guys! I don't want to talk about the game anymore."

# Chapter 10

"Are you coming to our game tonight, Mom?" inquired Toby as he grabbed his gym shorts from the dryer.

"I'm going to try, Toby. I'm going to the hospital after work........... I'll try to stop by if I can."

"Maybe you could video-tape the game for Dad!"

"We'll see, Toby.......... I don't want to cause any stress for your dad. He's only awake about an hour a day.......... I don't think he wants to watch a basketball game............I mean............"

"Never mind. I'll see you tonight, Mom!"

"Toby, wait! ....... Eat your breakfast .......... Toby!"

Toby's mom caught the screen door as he

jumped off the deck and headed towards the bus stop.

*"Doesn't anybody care about my basketball game?"* mumbled Toby as he shoved two breakfast bars in his gym bag. *"Does anyone know what it's been like the last week at school? All I've heard is how I missed the last shot. Now, my own family doesn't want to come to my game."*

"Toby, who are you talking to?" questioned Jordan.

"Where'd you come from?" replied Toby.

"We always meet at the stop every day……… What's wrong?... Are you sick? You're not going to miss the game tonight are you?"

"It's not like you guys need me on the team, Jordan. I'll probably just mess up anyway! Coach probably won't even play me tonight!"

"I'm sure you'll play, Toby!"

"I don't know; the Buffaloes are tough!"

"Coach plays everyone, no matter how good

they are!"

"What do you mean by that?"

"I didn't mean anything. It just came out wrong," stammered Jordan.

"It doesn't matter. I'll talk to you later......... I'm going to walk to school today."

Toby threw his bag over his left shoulder and began his twenty minute hike to school.

*"I have to prove myself tonight.............I have to show everyone that I belong out there...........It's always been the four of us ever since fourth grade........ Now all of a sudden I'm not good enough............ I've got to focus....................I can feel it...... Tonight is my night!"*

Buzz! Buzz!

"Excuse the interruption students. We have one announcement before the end of the day. We want to wish the Stars good luck tonight against the Buffaloes. This will be their second conference game of the season! Go.........Stars........!"

"Toby, I'll see you on the court! Coach wants us out there twenty minutes early to go through some new plays," interrupted David.

"Did you know about that, Jeremiah?" questioned Toby as he closed his English book and stashed it in his backpack.

"Yeah, Coach told us last night at practice."

"I don't remember him saying that."

"It's no big deal; I'll see you out there."

The Stars took the court twenty minutes before game time to warm up. Meantime the Buffaloes were at the opposite end of the court sporting their calisthenics for the crowd.

"They look big," bellowed Jeremiah.

"I know. They're bigger than David," Reggie responded as he threw the ball to Toby.

Toby focused his warm up shots at the spot that he missed the game-winning basket the week before, but he still couldn't hit the net. After he missed for the fifth time in a row, the horn sounded signaling that it was time to start the game. Everyone sprinted to their respective benches, except for Toby who walked, gazing straight at the ground. As the team gathered in the huddle, Toby scanned the crowd for his mom.

"Welcome to the Stars Territory. Now, for the starting line-up for your Saben's Stars. Starting at center...at 6'1"..... David Smith. At forward....at 5'8"......Reggie Loring. At the other forward....... at 5'10"......Jordan Crip. At guard.....at 5'6".... Jeremiah Nestle. And at the other guard........ at 5'5".......Jared Duke."

The team took to the center circle as Toby and the other boys took to the bench.

The referee threw the ball into the air and David controlled it to Reggie. Reggie passed it back to David; he drove into the lane and made a lay-up. Everyone jumped up from the bench with fists wailing in the air, except Toby. The first half passed quickly without Toby moving off of his designated spot on the end of the bench. The team sprinted into the locker room down seven at the half.

"I'm going to change the line-up for the second half," announced Coach Jensen.

Toby's head shot up to see what names he was writing on the chalkboard, but once again, his name was not mentioned, and his head went back down to the ground.

The third quarter started identical to the first quarter with David hitting a lay-up. David scored ten points in a row for the Stars, and all of a sudden, they took the lead. They kept the lead all the way into the fourth quarter when the score was 42-37 in the Stars favor with a minute and a half to go. Suddenly Coach stood up from his seat and looked down the bench and yelled out, "Toby, go check in." Toby couldn't believe it; he was actually going to get into the game. He took his red warm-up jacket off and ran to the scorer's bench and checked in his number. He scanned the crowd one more time.

"Toby!....Toby!...." screamed a frail voice from the fourth row under the basket.

Toby painted a grin from ear-to-ear as he waited to enter the game. David took the ball at the top of the key.

"Run the spread offense!" belted Coach from the bench. The clock continued to run. The seconds kept ticking away while Toby was still waiting anxiously to get into the game. David and Reggie continued running and passing the ball sporadically trying to tire the Buffalo defense.

"Five…Four…Three…Two…One...!" chanted the crowd.

The buzzer went off. The Stars had upset the number one team in the conference. Toby got up from the floor in front of the scorer's bench and joined the team victory huddle amidst the jubilant crowd of parents.

"Good job tonight, boys! That's the kind of hustle and team work I've been talking about. You guys played like a team. Good effort on everyone's part! We'll see you tomorrow at practice."

"Coach!"

"Yes, Toby."

"Can I talk to you for a minute?"

"Sure, what can I do for you?..........Has something happened to your dad?"

"No,.................I was just wondering........ ah..."

"Go ahead, Toby."

"Well, ...I didn't get in tonight........... I always started in sixth grade. I don't understand!"

"Toby, you're a great kid. You're the type of player every coach hopes to have on their team. You have a good attitude and you always give 100 percent in practice and in the game........ Right now, we can really use David's height. This was a big game tonight……."

"Yeah, I know. I understand………Thanks, Coach."

"We'll see you at practice tomorrow, Toby."

Toby grabbed his towel and warm-up jacket and splintered his way through the lingering crowd of parents towards the locker room.

"Toby!"

Toby paused and shot a glance over his right shoulder towards the north basket.

"Mom!" shouted Toby over the chorus of chatter.

Toby jostled his way across the center line towards his mom at the north end of the gym.

"Great game tonight! I got the second half on tape for your dad."

"Mom, I didn't even get in the game! Dad's not going to want to watch a game that I'm not even playing."

"Toby, your team won. Your dad will want to

see the game!"

"Mom, I started all last year. Now, I'm hardly getting to play......... It's a good thing dad isn't here."

"I don't want to hear you talk like that ever again, Toby. Now, go get dressed. I'd like to stop by the hospital on the way home....... I'll meet you out in the front circle in ten minutes."

"I'm sorry, Mom. I didn't mean to say anything bad about Dad............. Are you going to show him the tape tonight?"

"No, he's probably asleep. I'll save it for when he gets home."

"Is he ever going to come home?"...............

# Chapter 11

Toby poked his head through the gaping doors and bounded quickly off the elevator.

"Come on, Mom!"

"Toby, you're going the wrong way. They moved your dad to a different room."

"Is he still on the fifth floor?"

"Yes, he's down here to the left. Just follow the yellow tiles."

Toby meandered timidly through the dimly lit hallway with his mom. He perused each room as he cross-stepped every tile in his path.

"Mom, it's really quiet up here tonight. What's going on?"

"Most of these patients require special care, like your dad."

"Doesn't anybody talk?..... Where's all of the doctors and nurses?...... It's kind of creepy!"

"Toby, your dad's room is up here on the left. Before we go in, there's something you should know."

Toby reared back and flattened himself against the wall waiting for his mother to finish her sentence. "What's wrong now? I thought Dad was doing better?"

"Your dad's left side is not responding!"

"Not responding to what?" questioned Toby as he threw his baseball cap to the floor.

"The trauma to your dad's head has left him temporarily paralyzed on the left side. His speech has been affected, as well. He may fully recover or he might not..........The doctor's just don't know at this point."

"When did all of this happen? .............How come nobody told me?"

"Toby, I spent the whole day here with your

dad. I didn't want to upset you before the big game. Your dad insisted."

Toby's eyes lit up as he realized what his mom had just said.

"You mean Dad talked to you today?...... He's awake?.......Did he tell you to video-tape my game?"

"Yes, Toby. You know how your dad loves the game! He wouldn't miss you playing for the world!"

"Is he still awake?.....Can I talk to him tonight?"

Mrs. Fields smiled as she put her hand on her son's shoulder and nudged him towards the doorway of room 511. Toby tapped gently on the door and waited for a reply. He paused and tapped again as he inched his way into the room. He paused again drawing closer to his dad's bedside. Toby glanced back at his mom and got the nod to approach his dad.

"Dad, it's me, Toby."

Toby waited for something to happen as he picked up the green armchair from the corner of the room and parked it next to the bed.

"T..i..o..b..y..!"

"Dad, you're awake!! You said my name!!...........Mom he's talking!" Toby couldn't contain his excitement. He grabbed his dad's hand and held it under his left arm like a basketball. Mrs. Fields nestled her head on his shoulders and kissed his cheek gently. Struggling to speak, his dad managed to slip Toby a grin through his crusted upper lip. Toby snatched a wash cloth from the bed table, dipped one corner into his dad's water cup, and gently swabbed his dad's lips.

Toby suddenly broke the silence.

"I can't take this anymore....... Dad, when are you coming home? ......It's been four weeks." Toby dropped his dad's hand and jumped up out of the chair. "We only have four games left........

You have to make it to at least one!"

"Toby, that's enough. Sit down!" demanded his mom as she grabbed the remote control.

Toby sat down and watched his mom burrow through her purse.

"What are you looking for?" Toby asked inquisitively.

"Remember our surprise!"

Toby scratched his left ear and threw his mom a bamboozled look as she drew from her purse the black cartridge. Sweat drops began to trickle down his forehead as he realized the surprise.

"I don't know if Dad's up to seeing the game right now……. He looks a little tired," Toby responded shamefacedly.

"I think this is just what your dad needs!"

"P..i..t t… g..e..m….n..," muttered Toby's dad eagerly.

Toby sprawled out in his chair with his head tilted over the back as his mom hit the play button.

"I can't believe I have to watch this game again!" mumbled Toby under his breath.

"W..a..t.. a s…h…a..t! T..i..o..b..y. , h..o..o..s.. t..h..e..t k…d…?"

Toby rolled his eyes and turned towards his dad as he wadded up his cap in his hands. "His name is David. He's a new kid at our school............He's okay, I guess."

"L..o…o…k..s l…i..k. h..e..s. y..o..r m...a..n," Toby's dad responded with a spark of excitement in his voice.

Toby sank further in his chair as the fourth quarter rolled around.

"H…o…w c..u…m y…o…r n…t p..l… a..i..n..g, T..i..o…b..y?"

Toby glanced over at his mom as he groped for the right answer.

"There are a lot of guards this year……… The coach has been subbing in and out every game."

"I've noticed that too, Toby," echoed his mom.

Toby returned a grin to his mom as he sat back up in his chair and fluffed his dad's pillow. "Dad!...Dad!.... Mom, what's wrong with dad?.... He won't answer me!"

"It looks like he's out again, Toby. He sleeps a lot right now."

"Why was he talking so weird?"

"I told you that his one side is paralyzed. Remember, I said his speech has been affected, too."

"Will he ever talk right again?"

"Well, Toby, there's no guarantee."

Toby paused and walked over to the television and ejected the basketball tape.

"I'm going to leave this for him in case he wants to watch it again tomorrow."

"I'm sure he would like that.......... Let's go home... It's been a long day for all of us."

# Chapter 12

"Good Morning, Toby!"

"Hey, Mr. Lee!"

"What are you doing here so early?"

"Ah...I thought I'd get in a few shots before school this morning. I'm meeting some of the guys in the gym at 7:30."

"Oh, that's right. Tonight's the last game."

"Are you coming?"

"Yes, I plan on being there. I wouldn't miss it!" exclaimed Mr. Lee.

"Great! ......Well....I better go... The guys are probably waiting."

"Miss Foley informed us that your dad might be coming home in a week! That's great news!"

"Yeah!...Hopefully he'll be home in time for

Thanksgiving next week."

"How's he doing?"

"Ah...he's walking now, but he still has to use a walker. His left side still isn't working quite right...He's talking better, though!"

"Hey, Toby," interrupted Reggie as he skidded to an abrupt stop in front of the science lab. "We've been waiting for you."

"Hey, Reggie! Ah....I've got to get going....... See you in class, Mr. Lee."

"See you later, boys!"

"So, are you ready for tonight's game? This is the last game before our conference tournament."

"I guess.....I probably won't get in much."

"Toby, you don't even act like you like basketball anymore. What's up?"

"I don't know....it's just....well....now that David moved to town, I don't get to play much. I know he's good and all, but it's always been us four. Remember how awesome fifth grade basketball was? We dominated! We went undefeated that year. Last year, nobody could touch us. It's just not the same this year. I'm just not feeling it............ I don't really feel like shooting this morning. I've got to get to class. I'll catch you later."

"Hey, Toby!"

"Oh,... hi,... Alyssa! Can't talk.........gotta' get to class!"

"Reggie, what's wrong with Toby? He didn't even look at me just now."

"I don't know. He's been acting really weird lately."

"What do you mean?"

"You know. He's just not the old Toby. He doesn't even like basketball anymore."

"That doesn't sound like Toby. He loves basketball."

"Maybe you can talk to him, Alyssa."

"What do you want me to say?"

"I don't know. Just cheer him up. He's got to

be ready for the game tonight."

"How's his dad?...... Is he home yet?"

"I don't know for sure. He doesn't talk about him much...... He's just not the same Toby!"

Reggie and Alyssa left the gym corridor as the first bell sounded.

*"Would Toby Fields please report to the office!"*

Reggie and Alyssa paused momentarily as they heard Toby's name being blasted over the intercom.

"I'll catch you later, Alyssa; I'm going to the office."

"I'm going, too," echoed Alyssa as the two of them sprinted towards the main office.

By the time Alyssa and Reggie got to the office, Toby was already in Miss Foley's office behind closed doors.

"May I help you, Reggie?" inquired Ms. Porter, the school secretary.

"Ah.....we were just wondering about

Toby.........we heard his name.........and....ah .....we just wanted to see him."

"I think you should probably get to class. The tardy bell rings in two minutes."

"Will you let him know we're out here?" Reggie pleaded with his hands plastered on the front desk.

"Reggie, Toby will be fine. Now, please, go to class before the two of you are tardy."

"Come on, Reggie; let's go before we're late."

"I don't know why we can't wait for him........ Something might be really wrong," bellowed Reggie slamming the office door shut.

"You better go on to class, Alyssa. I'm going to sit out here on the bench and wait for Toby. I'll see you later."

Reggie sat edgily waiting for Toby to emerge from the office.

"*What's he's doing in there?*" Reggie mumbled under his breath.

"Reggie, what are you doing out here? Did you get in trouble again?"

"Trouble........? I've been waiting on you for the last fifteen minutes. What's going on?"

"Oh, nothing really," smirked Toby.

You were in there for an awfully long time for nothing. What happened?" persisted Reggie.

"You'll see tonight!" exclaimed Toby.

"See what?"

"I'll catch you later. Thanks for waiting for me! I've got to get to class."

"Since when do you worry about class? .......Toby, where are you going?...... Tell me what's going on!..... I can't wait all day to find out!"

# Chapter 13

"Alright, boys, this is our last game before the conference tournament next week and we need a win! Don't forget what we have talked about all year. Remember the fundamentals; now let's go get 'em!"

The Stars charged the court eagerly after Coach Jensen's speech and hastily lined up as everyone stood for the National Anthem.

"Welcome to the Star's Territory. The Stars enter the last game of the regular season with a record of 8-1. Now, for the starting line-up for your Saben's Stars. Starting at center…at 6'1"….. David Smith. At forward….at 5'8"……Reggie Loring. At the other forward…….at 5'10"…… Jordan Crip. At guard…..at 5'6"….Jeremiah

Nestle. And at the other guard........ at 5'5"....... Jared Duke."

The boys clasped hands and took to center court as Toby took to his usual starting spot on the bench. The Warren Wizards controlled the tip and immediately drove to the basket and were fouled on the way up by David. Both free throws were good and the Wizards were off to an early lead. Reggie quickly in-bounded the ball to David. David took it coast to coast and went up for the lay-up. The crowd stood on their feet in awe as a charging foul was called on the play, which made two fouls for David in less than twenty seconds. Coach Jensen signaled David to the bench.

"What are you doing out there? Use your head........Whatever you do don't pick up your third foul!"

The first quarter ended with a tie game at thirteen. The Wizards had the possession arrow so they controlled the ball to begin the second quarter. The crowd watched as the Wizards duplicated the beginning of the game with a quick three-pointer from the arch. David seized the ball and threw it in to Jordan at mid-court. Jordan leaped into the air to snatch the pass, but it was picked off by the Wizards who made a quick lay-up to go up by another two. The Wizards continued their momentum and increased their lead throughout the quarter. With eleven seconds to go, they were up seven with the ball for a chance at a last second play. The Wizards threw in the ball and went into a brief stall before throwing a perfect pass to the center offender directly under the basket. David vaulted straight up to block the shot but a foul was called and the Wizards made the basket. The free throw was good. The Wizards took a ten point lead going into half-time. The crowd stood to their feet and cheered the Stars on as they sprinted into the locker room.

"I only have one thing to say, guys," Coach

Jensen heralded as he walked over to the chalkboard. "DEFENSE!"

Coach Jensen walked out of the locker room without saying another word.

"I know we can do this, guys..... We've had a great season..... We can't end it this way......David, we really need you out there!...........Everybody, ONE, TWO, THREE, TEAM!!" shouted Toby as he led the players out of the locker room.

"Good speech, Toby."

"Thanks, Reggie," beamed Toby as he scanned the crowd during warm-ups.

"Who are you looking for?"

"Oh, I was just seeing who was in the crowd."

"Is your mom here tonight?"

"I don't know; I haven't seen her yet!"

As the boys gathered in their huddle, the crowd stood to their feet and began clapping and chanting, "GO Stars, Go Stars, Go Stars!!"

Suddenly the chanting stopped.

"Toby, look!"

"What?"

"It's your parents!"

"Where?.....Where are they?"

Suddenly the gym broke out in a euphoric salute as Toby's dad shuffled into the gym through the north doors.

Toby stood speechless, fighting back tears, while he watched his dad walk slowly over to the first row bleachers behind the visitor's bench. Jeremiah pulled Toby into the huddle and gripped his left hand tightly.

"This game's for Toby!" screamed Jeremiah above the cheering crowd as he sprinted to center court for the start of the third quarter.

Toby took his place on the bench as the third quarter began. The Stars appeared to be on a mission; they went on a 12-0 run to start the quarter to regain the lead by 2 points. The Wizards quickly called a time out to stop the driving momentum of the Stars.

"Great defense, boys!........ That's what we've been talking about..........Jeremiah, keep up those screens....... Reggie, watch your man under the basket........... David, you're doing a great job going to the basket......Keep it up....... Alright,...... ONE, TWO, THREE, TEAM!"

"Jordan, what's wrong with Toby?"

"What do you think, Smith?" Jordan muttered as the boys headed back onto the court.

David knew what he needed to do as he glanced back at Toby on the end of the bench. As the Stars took the court, David deliberately darted to the nearest opponent and grabbed him to get an intentional foul.

"David, what are you doing?" shrieked Coach Jensen flapping his hands in the air from the sidelines.

With only twenty seconds left in the third quarter, David signaled Reggie to throw him the ball mid-court. Reggie heaved the ball as David charged into the Wizard's defender knocking him to the ground. Coach Jensen jumped to his feet in disbelief as David came to the sidelines with his fifth foul.

"Toby, you're in!" belted Coach Jensen in fury.

Toby tore off his warm-ups and dashed to the scorer's bench with a smile plastered to his face. The Stars in-bounded the ball with twenty seconds left on the clock. Jordan nailed a three pointer to tie the game at 41 at the end of the third quarter.

As the third quarter horn sounded, the crowd rose to their feet and began chanting, "GO STARS, GO STARS, GO........... STARS!!!!"

"Here we go, boys........This is it............... Toby, you'll be playing the four spot."

"But, Coach, I'm not a forward. I've never played that position."

"Toby, you're a forward!...........Now let's get out there and play basketball!"

The Stars had possession to start the fourth quarter. Toby seized the ball on the wing, took one dribble around his man, and dribbled it off his foot out-of -bounds.

"Settle down, Toby," Jordan mumbled as he patted Toby on the back.

The Wizards dribbled the ball up the court where Toby was waiting at the top of the key. As the Wizard guard made a move to the left, Toby stripped the ball away and zipped down the court for a lay-up; his first points of the season. His face gleamed as he raced back down the court to his defending position. The game continued to go back and forth for most of the last quarter until the Wizards called a timeout with 1:34 remaining, trailing by just one point.

"Great effort out there, Toby!....That's the kind of hustle I like to see.........Reggie, Jeremiah...

they're probably going to take it inside.....Jordan, watch the wing........Alright, boys....this is it!"

"Thanks, David," Toby whispered as they broke out of the huddle.

"Not a problem......., Go get 'em!" David replied with a grin as he took his position on the bench.

As the horn sounded, the entire gym echoed with cheers of excitement. The players took the court for the conclusion of the game. The Wizards quickly brought the ball up the court and went into a stall pattern, trying to wait for the last shot. They passed it around the top of the key for over a minute, before synchronizing their set play. The Wizard point guard dribbled it into the lane, kicked it out to their shooter, and put up a three pointer...IT WAS GOOD! Jordan immediately signaled for a timeout. They had seven seconds to attempt a shot and a chance to win the game.

As the team gathered together for one final

huddle, Coach Jensen stood up and pulled out his clipboard.

"Ok, .....listen carefully. Jordan, this play is yours. Toby, you need to get Jordan the ball as soon as you get to the corner. This is it, guys, team on three....ONE, TWO, THREE...TEAM!"

Toby broke out of the huddle and caught his dad's eye across the court. They both exchanged a quick nod and glanced up at the score board as the team took the court.

"Relax, Toby," Jordan whispered reassuringly smacking Toby on the back.

Toby took the inbound pass as the coach had designed and scurried up the court. Jordan had three guys pinned to him and Reggie was trapped on the sideline.

"Throw the ball to Jeremiah," yelled Coach Jensen from the bench.

"FOUR," chanted the crowd.

"Over here, Toby. Pass it!" screamed Reggie

over the roar of the fans.

"THREE!"

"SHOOT!" screeched David from the bench.

"SHOOT, Toby! You can do it!" squealed Alyssa from the cheer block.

"TWO....ONE!"

Toby pivoted around on his right foot and threw up a 30-footer from the arch as the horn blasted.............

# Chapter 14

"That was quite a game tonight, son. Everyone was definitely on the edge of their seats during those last seven seconds........... I'm very proud of you.........You gave it your all.......I wouldn't have missed it for anything!"

"Yeah, I was pretty nervous.........I wasn't sure whether the shot was in or not!" Toby countered as he walked over to the couch and sat between his mom and dad.

Toby's dad pulled him close to his side while extending his left arm back behind the couch.

"What are you doing, Dad?"

"I have something for you!........... Coach Jensen wanted me to give this to you!"

"Give me what?" grilled Toby as he peered

behind the couch.

"He wanted me to present you with the team ball. The team voted unanimously that you deserved it after tonight's performance."

Toby stood speechless as he embraced the ball tightly against his chest with both hands. "I think this ball belongs to both of us, Dad!" sniveled Toby as he gave the autographed ball back to his dad.

"I don't know what to say...........I know this has been a long ordeal for both of you........I'm thankful to be here................................ " Toby's dad pulled his wife and son closer to him, embracing them both.

Toby's eyes bloated with tears as he realized that he had a lot to be thankful for, as well: good friends, the basketball team, winning the game, his mom, but most of all, his dad's life. It was indeed a day to give thanks!